IMAGINE

Alison Lester

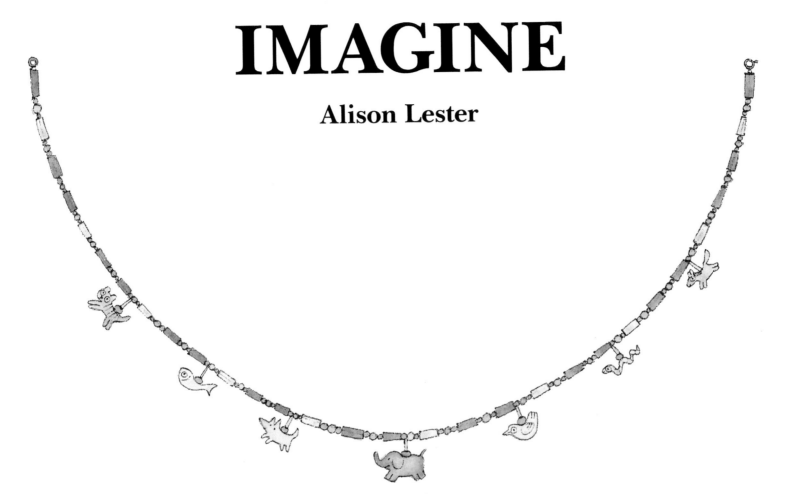

For Rich and Bee

VIKING

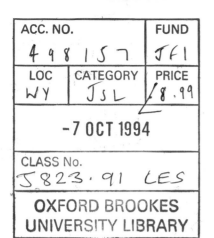
Imagine
if we were
deep in the jungle
where butterflies drift
and jaguars prowl
where parakeets squawk
and wild monkeys howl . . .

■

anaconda • tree frog • paca • hummingbird • toucan • three-toed sloth • butterfly • macaw • jagua

scarlet ibis • butterfly

spider monkey • cayman • peccary • giant armadillo

• twist-necked turtle • water cavy • piranha • boa constrictor • howler monkey • spider monkey • cayman f-cutter ant • harpy eagle • vampire bat • marsh deer • cock-of-the-rock • giant anteater • ocelot

murine opossum • tamandua • tapir • fresh-water dolphin • porcupine

ary • giant armadillo • scarlet ibis • bird-eating spider • butterfly • macaw • jaguar • leaf-cutter ant • tapir

Imagine
if we were
like fish in the ocean
where anemones wave
and hammerheads glide
where seahorses rock
and hermit crabs hide . . .

■

ale • hermit crab • sawfish • butterfly fish • giant clam • angelfish • angler fish • sea-snake • sponge

sea-dragon • hammerhead shark • prawn • starfish • moray eel • stingray

ying fish • trumpet-fish • swordfish • flounder • moorish idol • limpet • clownfish • anemone • oyster •

Imagine
if we were
crossing the icecap
where penguins toboggan
and arctic hares dash
where caribou snort
and killer whales crash . . .

■

husky • arctic wolf • musk ox • arctic tern • snow goose • albatross • caribou • adele penguin • sn

arctic hare • adele penguin • arctic dolphin • narwhal • humpback whale

•puffin • elephant seal • emperor penguin • loon • lemming • sea lion • harp seal • guillemot • kittiwa

wl • arctic squirrel • walrus • harp seal • guillemot • kittiwake • herring • polar bear • beluga whale •

killer whale • humpback whale • narwhal • arctic dolphin • arctic hare

umpback whale • narwhal • arctic dolphin • husky • adele penguin • snowy owl • arctic squirrel • loon

Imagine
if we were
out in the country
where horses gallop
and cattle graze
where turkeys gobble
and sheepdogs laze . . .

■

bull • cow • calf • cat • kitten • stockhorse • foal • pony • draughthorse • sheepdog • puppy • sheep • g

foal • pig • goat • cockatoo • swan • cat • calf • piglet • drake • sheep • turkey

• cockatoo • goat • draughthorse • sheepdog • puppy • sheep • drake • duckling • rabbit • pig • roos

Imagine
if we were
surrounded by monsters
where pteranodons swoop
and triceratops smash
where stegosaurs stomp
and tyrannosaurs gnash . . .

■

Imagine
if we were
away on safari
where crocodiles lurk
and antelope feed
where leopards attack
and zebras stampede . . .

∎

Imagine
if we were
alone in the moonlight
where bandicoots nibble
and wallabies jump
where wombats dig burrows
and kangaroos thump . . .

■

Imagine
if we had
our own little house
with a cat on the bed
a rug on the floor
a light in the night
and a dog at the door . . .

■

Imagine . . .

∎

VIKING

Published by the Penguin Group
Penguin Books Ltd, 27 Wrights Lane, London W8 5TZ, England
Viking Penguin, a division of Penguin Books USA Inc.
375 Hudson Street, New York, New York 10014, USA
Penguin Books Australia Ltd, Ringwood, Victoria, Australia
Penguin Books Canada Ltd, 2801 John Street, Markham, Ontario, Canada L3R 1B4
Penguin Books (NZ) Ltd, 182–190 Wairau Road, Auckland 10, New Zealand

Penguin Books Ltd, Registered Offices: Harmondsworth, Middlesex, England

First published by Allen & Unwin Australia Pty Ltd 1989
First published in Great Britain by Viking 1991
1 3 5 7 9 10 8 6 4 2

Printed in Singapore by Imago

A CIP catalogue record for this book is available from the British Library
ISBN 0-670-83692 3